'He was blamed for endless disasters, from failed exams to a bridge collapse, an avalanche, even a shipwreck: all due, in the stupid opinion of, first, his fellow-students and, later, his colleagues, to the penetrating power of his evil eye…'

PRIMO LEVI
Born 31 July 1919, Turin
Died 11 April 1987, Turin

'The Death of Marinese' (1949), 'Censorship in Bitinia'
(1961), 'Knall' (1968–70), 'The Magic Paint' (1973),
'Gladiators' (1976), 'The Fugitive' (1979), 'Bureau of Vital
Statistics' (1981) and 'Buffet Dinner' (1977) first published
in English in book form in *A Tranquil Star*, 2007.

ALSO PUBLISHED BY PENGUIN BOOKS
The Periodic Table · *Moments of Reprieve* · *If Not Now, When?* ·
A Tranquil Star

PRIMO LEVI

The Magic Paint

TRANSLATED BY ANN GOLDSTEIN,
ALESSANDRA BASTAGLI AND
JENNY MCPHEE

PENGUIN BOOKS

PENGUIN CLASSICS

Published by the Penguin Group
Penguin Books Ltd, 80 Strand, London WC2R ORL, England
Penguin Group (USA), Inc., 375 Hudson Street, New York, New York 10014, USA
Penguin Group (Canada), 90 Eglinton Avenue East, Suite 700, Toronto, Ontario,
Canada M4P 2Y3 (a division of Pearson Penguin Canada Inc.)
Penguin Ireland, 25 St Stephen's Green, Dublin 2, Ireland (a division of Penguin Books Ltd)
Penguin Group (Australia), 250 Camberwell Road, Camberwell, Victoria 3124, Australia
(a division of Pearson Australia Group Pty Ltd)
Penguin Books India Pvt Ltd, 11 Community Centre, Panchsheel Park,
New Delhi - 110 017, India
Penguin Group (NZ), 67 Apollo Drive, Rosedale, North Shore 0632, New Zealand
(a division of Pearson New Zealand Ltd)
Penguin Books (South Africa) (Pty) Ltd, 24 Sturdee Avenue, Rosebank, Johannesburg 2196,
South Africa
Penguin Books Ltd, Registered Offices: 80 Strand, London WC2R ORL, England

www.penguin.com

Selected from *A Tranquil Star* published in Penguin Classics 2007
This selection published in Penguin Classics 2011

1

Copyright © W. W. Norton & Company, Inc., 2007
Translation copyright © Ann Goldstein and Alessandra Bastagli, 2007
'Censorship in Bitinia' translation copyright © Jenny McPhee, 2007

Typeset by Jouve (UK), Milton Keynes
Printed in England by Clays Ltd, St Ives plc

ISBN: 978-0-141-19609-1

www.greenpenguin.co.uk

Penguin Books is committed to a sustainable future
for our business, our readers and our planet.
The book in your hands is made from paper
certified by the Forest Stewardship Council.

Mixed Sources
Product group from well-managed
forests and other controlled sources
www.fsc.org Cert no. SA-COC-1592
© 1996 Forest Stewardship Council

FSC

Contents

The Magic Paint

For many years now I have been engaged in the manufacture of paints and, more precisely, their formulation: from this art I earn my sustenance and support my family. It's an ancient and noble art: the earliest reference appears in Genesis 6:14, where it is related how, in obedience to an exact specification on the part of the Almighty, Noah (probably using a brush) covered the Ark, inside and out, with pitch. But it's also a subtly fraudulent art, which tends to hide the substratum, endowing it with the color and the appearance of what it is not: in this it is related to the arts of makeup and costume, which are equally equivocal and equally ancient (Isaiah 3:16 ff).

The most varied demands are constantly being made on those who practice this profession of ours: paints that do not conduct electricity and paints that do, paints that transmit heat or reflect it, that keep mollusks from adhering to hulls, that absorb sound, or that can be removed from a surface like a peel from a banana. People require paints that keep feet from slipping, as for airport steps, and others as slippery as possible, as for the bottoms of skis. We are therefore a versatile people, with vast experience, who are accustomed to both success and the lack of it, and are difficult to surprise.

Nonetheless, we were surprised by a request that came from our agent in Naples, Signor Amato Di Prima: he was pleased to inform us that an important client in his area had experimented with a paint that provided protection from misfortune, and would profitably replace horn amulets, hunchbacks, four-leaf clovers, and charms in general. It had not been possible to glean other information, except for the price, which was very high; he had, however, managed to obtain a sample, which he had already sent by mail. Given the exceptional interest of the product, he urgently beseeched us to devote the greatest attention to the problem, declared his faith in a quick response, and extended his most sincere greetings.

This business, of the miraculous sample that arrives in the mail, along with an urgent prayer to devote et cetera (that is, without resorting to euphemism, to copy it), is part of our work, and constitutes perhaps its most obscure aspect. We would like to do things our own way: make our own choice, of a refined and elegant problem, take off on the hunt, sight the solution, pursue it, corner it, spear it, strip it of everything inessential, make it in the laboratory, then manufacture it on a small scale, and finally go into full production and get money and glory from it. But that almost never happens. There are many of our kind in this world, and our colleagues and rivals in Italy, in America, in Australia, in Japan are not exactly dozing. We are awash in samples, and we would happily yield to the temptation to throw them away or return them to the sender, were it not for the consideration that our own products suffer the same fate, becoming, in their turn, marvelous, being shrewdly seized and smuggled out by the agents of our competitors, scrutinized, analyzed, and copied: some badly, others well – by the addition, that is, of a particle of originality and genius. Thus begins an endless network of espionage and cross-fertilization, which, illuminated by solitary creative flashes, constitutes the foundation of technological progress. In short, the samples of the competition cannot be thrown out with the dregs: one must see what's there, even if the professional conscience puts up a struggle.

The paint that came from Naples, at first glance, did not display any special property: appearance, odor, drying time were those of a common clear acrylic enamel, and the whole business stank of a hoax. I telephoned Di

Prima, who was indignant: he was not the type to send samples around just for fun, and that one in particular had cost him time and trouble – the product was extremely interesting and in his market he was having incredible success. Technical documentation? It didn't exist, there was no need for it, the effectiveness of the product spoke for itself. A fishing boat had been coming back with empty nets for three months – they had painted its hull and ever since it had been netting spectacular catches. A typographer had mixed the paint with printing ink: the ink didn't go as far, but the typographical errors had disappeared. If somehow we were unable to use it, we should tell him immediately; otherwise, we should get busy with it. The price was 7000 lire a kilo, which seemed to him a good profit margin, and he would undertake to sell at least twenty tons a month.

I talked about it with Chiovatero, who is a serious and capable fellow. At first he turned up his nose, then he thought about it, and proposed starting simply; that is, trying the paint on cultures of *E. coli* bacteria. What did he expect? That the cultures would multiply more than the controls or less? Chiovatero was annoyed, and told me that it was not his habit to put the cart before the horse (implying, by this, that it was *my* habit, which, for goodness' sake, is absolutely not true), that it remained to be seen, that you had to start somewhere, and that 'the load adjusts along the way.' He obtained the cultures, painted the outside of the test tubes, and we waited. None of us were biologists, but no biologist was needed to interpret the results. After five days, the effect was obvious: the protected cultures had developed in size at three times the rate of the controls, which we had coated with an acrylic ostensibly similar to the one from Naples. We had to conclude that this paint 'brought good luck' even to microorganisms: an irritating conclusion, but, as has been authoritatively stated, facts are obstinate. A more thorough analysis was required, but everyone knows what a complex and uncertain enterprise the examination of a paint is: almost like that of a living organism. All those fantastic modern devices – the infrared spectrum, the gas chromatograph, NMR – are helpful to a point but leave many angles unexplored; and if you aren't lucky enough to have a metal as the key component, all you can do is use your nose, like a dog. But in this case there *was* a metal: an unusual metal, so unusual that no one in the laboratory knew from experience how it reacted. We had to burn almost the entire sample to obtain a quantity sufficient for identification; but finally we did and it was duly confirmed, with all its characteristic reactions. It was tantalum, a very respectable metal, with a name full of meaning, never before seen in paint, and thus surely responsible for the property that we were looking for. As always happens once you've made a finding and confirmed it, the presence of tantalum, and its specific function, began to seem gradually less strange, and, finally, natural, just as no one is surprised anymore by X rays. Molino pointed out that the most acid-resistant reaction vessels are made with tantalum; Palazzoni recalled that tantalum is used to make surgical prostheses that absolutely can't be rejected; and so we concluded that it is an obviously beneficial metal, and that we had been foolish to waste so much time on analyses. With a little common sense we should have been able to think of it right off.

In a few days we got a soap of tantalum, put it in some paint, and tried it on the *E. coli*: it worked, the goal was achieved.

We, in turn, sent a large sample of paint to Di Prima, so that he could distribute it to his customers and give us an opinion. The opinion arrived two months later, and was highly favorable: he, Di Prima, had painted himself from head to foot, and then had spent four hours under a ladder, on a Friday, in the company of thirteen black cats, without coming to any harm. Chiovatero also tried it, albeit reluctantly (not because he was superstitious; rather because he was skeptical), and he had to admit that a certain effect was undeniable: in the two or three days after the treatment, all the traffic lights he came to were green, he never got a busy signal on the telephone, his girlfriend made up with him, and he even won a modest prize in the lottery. Naturally it all came to an end after he took a bath.

As for me, I thought of Michele Fassio. Fassio is an old schoolmate of mine to whom mysterious powers had been attributed since adolescence. He was blamed for endless disasters, from failed exams to a bridge collapse, an avalanche, even a shipwreck: all due, in the stupid opinion of, first, his fellow-students and, later, his colleagues, to the penetrating power of his evil eye. I, of course, didn't believe this nonsense, but I confess that I often tried to avoid running into him. Fassio, poor fellow, ended up believing it himself, in a way; he never married and he led an unhappy life, of privation and solitude. I wrote to him, with all the delicacy I was capable of, that I didn't believe in this type of foolishness, but that he might; that, as a result, I couldn't believe in the remedy I was proposing, but it seemed to me that I owed it to him to mention it just the same, if only to help him recover his self-confidence. Fassio answered that he would come as soon as possible: he was willing to submit to a trial. Before proceeding with the treatment, and at the urging of Chiovatero, we tried to understand in some degree Fassio's powers. We managed to ascertain that in fact his gaze (and only his gaze) possessed a specific effect, noticeable under certain conditions even in the case of inanimate objects. We asked him to stare for several minutes at a particular point on a steel plate, which we then placed in the salt-spray chamber; after a few hours we noted that the point Fassio had stared at was clearly more corroded than the rest of the surface. A polyethylene thread, stretched tight, consistently broke at the point where Fassio's gaze hit it. To our satisfaction, both results disappeared when we coated the plate and the thread with our paint, or when we interposed between subject and object a glass screen previously coated with it. We were further able to ascertain that only Fassio's right eye was active: the left, like both of my eyes, and like Chiovatero's, exercised no measurable action. With the means at our disposal, we were unable to carry out a spectral analysis of the Fassio effect except in a crude way; it is probable, however, that the radiation under examination has a maximum in the blue, with a wavelength of around 425 Nm. Our exhaustive paper on the subject will be out in a few months. Now, it is known that many of those who wish to cast the evil eye wear blue-tinted lenses, and not dark ones, and this can't be a coincidence but must, rather, be the fruit of long experience absorbed perhaps unconsciously and then handed down from generation to generation, as in the case of certain folk remedies.

Considering the tragic conclusion of our tests, I have to explain that the idea of painting Fassio's eyeglasses (they were ordinary reading glasses) was neither mine nor Chiovatero's but came from Fassio himself, who insisted that the experiment be made right away, without even an hour's delay: he was very impatient to be released from his grim power. We painted these glasses. After thirty minutes the paint was dry: Fassio put them on and immediately fell lifeless at our feet. The doctor, who arrived soon afterward, tried in vain to revive him, and spoke vaguely of embolism, heart attack, and thrombosis: he couldn't have known that the lens over Fassio's right eye, concave on the inside, must have instantaneously reflected that thing which he could no longer transmit, and must have concentrated it, as if with a burning glass, on a point situated in some unspecified but important corner of the right cerebral hemisphere of the unhappy and blameless victim of our experiments.

The Death of Marinese

No one was killed. Sante and Marinese were the only ones captured by the Germans. It made no sense, it was almost incredible, that, of us all, the two of them had been taken. But the older men in the group knew that it is always those who are captured of whom it is later said 'Who would have guessed!' And they also knew why.

When the two were taken away, the sky was gray and the road was covered with snow that had hardened into ice. The truck barreled downhill with the engine off: the chains on the wheels rattled around the bends and clanked rhythmically along the straight stretches. About thirty Germans were standing in the back of the truck, packed shoulder to shoulder, some of them hanging onto the frame of the canvas roof. The tarp had come loose, so that a thin sleet struck their faces and came to rest on the fabric of their uniforms.

Sante was wounded; he sat mute and still on the rear bench of the truck, while Marinese was at the front, standing, with his back against the driver's cab. Trembling with fever, Marinese felt himself slowly overcome by a growing drowsiness, so that, taking advantage of a bump in the road, he slid to the wet floor and remained sitting there, an inanimate object amid the muddy boots, his bare head wedged between the bony hips of two soldiers.

The pursuit had been long and exhausting, and he wanted nothing more than this – for it all to be over, to remain sitting, to have no more decisions to make, to surrender to the heat of his fever and rest. He knew that he would be interrogated, probably beaten, and then almost certainly killed, and he knew, too, that soon all this would regain importance. But for now he felt strangely protected by a burning shield of fever and sleep, as if it were an insulation of cotton wool that separated him from the rest of the world, from the facts of the day and the things to come. Vacation, he thought, almost in a dream: how long had it been since he had had a vacation?

With his eyes closed, he felt as if he were submerged in a long, narrow tunnel that had been dug into a soft, tepid substance, crimson like the light that penetrates closed eyelids. His feet and his head were cold, and he seemed to be moving with difficulty, as if pushed, toward the exit, which was far away, but which he would finally, inexorably, reach. The exit was barred by a swirl of snow and a tangle of hard, frozen metal.

For Marinese a long time passed in this way, during which he made no attempt to break out of his cradle of fever. The truck reached the plain, and the Germans stopped to take off the chains. Then the drive resumed – faster, the jolts more violent.

Perhaps nothing would have happened if the Germans hadn't suddenly begun to sing. A voice, starting up in the cab, reached them muffled and indistinct. But once the first verse was over, a second burst forth like thunder from every chest, drowning out the rumble of the engine and the rush of the wind – even Marinese's fever was overwhelmed. He found himself again able to act and therefore, in some way, obliged to take action – which was how it was for all of us at that time.

The song was long; every verse ended abruptly, in the German manner, and the soldiers stamped twice on the wooden floor with their hobnailed boots. Marinese had opened his eyes and raised his head again, and every time they stamped their feet he perceived a light touch on his shoulder: he soon realized that it was the handle of a grenade, tucked diagonally into the belt of the man on his left. In that moment the idea took hold.

It's probable that, at least in the beginning, he hadn't considered using the grenade to save himself, to open up a path with his own hands, even though, as we shall see, his final actions cannot be interpreted otherwise. It's more likely that he was moved by hatred and rancor (feelings that had become habitual to us by then, almost an elementary reflex) toward those blond men in green, well nourished and well armed, who for many months had forced us to live in hiding. Perhaps more than that, he wanted to take revenge and yet at the same time cleanse himself of the shame of a final escape – the shame that weighed and still weighs on our souls. In fact, Marinese had a gentle soul, and none of us thought him capable of killing, except in self-defense, revenge, or anger.

Without turning his head, Marinese carefully groped for the handle of the grenade (the type shaped like a stick, with a timer) and, bit by bit, he unscrewed the safety cap, using the jolts of the vehicle to conceal his movements. This operation was easy enough, but Marinese never would have thought that it would be so difficult to occupy and get through the last ten seconds of his life – he would have to fight hard, with all his will and with all his physical strength, so that everything would go according to plan. He dedicated his last few moments to this alone: not to self-pity, not to the thought of God, not to taking leave of the memory of those he loved.

With the cord firmly in his grasp, Marinese tried to imagine, in an orderly fashion, what would happen in the ten seconds between the rip and the explosion. The Germans might not notice, might simply register his sudden movement, or might understand everything. The first option was the most favorable: the ten seconds would be his own, his time, to spend as he wished, perhaps to think of home, perhaps to think of how he would manage, taking shelter at the last minute behind the man on his right, but then he would have to count to ten and that thought was strangely worrisome. 'Fool,' he thought suddenly. 'Here I am racking my brains with the cord in my hand. I could have thought of it sooner, couldn't I. Now the first son of a bitch who sees the cap missing . . . But no, I can always pull, no matter what happens.' He laughed to himself: '(Even a situation like this has its advantages!) Even if they hit me in the back of the neck? Even if they shoot me?' . . . But yes, thanks to some mental mechanism, evidently illusory and distorted by the imminence of the decision, Marinese felt sure he could pull the cord no matter what, even the very instant he lost consciousness, perhaps even the instant after.

But unexpectedly, out of some unexplored depths, from some recess of his body – the animal, rebel body that has trouble deciding to die – something was born and grew beyond measure, something dark and primeval, and unfathomable, because its growth arrests and then replaces all the powers of knowledge and determination. It dawned on Marinese that this was fear, and he understood that, in a moment, it would be too late. He filled his lungs to prepare for battle and pulled the cord with all his might.

Rage was unleashed. A paw struck his shoulder, followed by an avalanche of bodies. But Marinese was able to tear the bomb away from the belt and roll up like a hedgehog, face down, his knees drawn up against his chest, the grenade wedged between his knees, his arms tight around them. The fierce blows of fists, musket butts, and heels rained down on his back; hard hands tried to violate the stronghold of his contracted limbs. But all in vain: it was not enough to overcome the insensitivity to pain and the primordial strength that, for just a few moments, nature grants us in a time of dire need.

For three or four seconds Marinese lay under a pile of bodies writhing in violent battle, every fiber of his being contracted. Then he heard the squeal of the brakes, the truck stopping, and the rushed thuds of men jumping to the ground. At that instant he sensed that the time had come. In a final, perhaps involuntary extension of all his powers, he tried, too late, to free himself of the grenade.

The explosion ripped apart the bodies of four Germans, and his own. Sante was executed by the Germans on the spot. The truck was abandoned, and we captured it the following night.

Censorship in Bitinia

I have already mentioned elsewhere the drab cultural life of this country, which is based, to this day, on a system of patronage and entrusted to the interests of the wealthy or even just to professionals and artists, specialists and technicians, who are quite well paid.

Of particular interest is the solution that was proposed for – or, to be more precise, that spontaneously imposed itself upon – the problem of censorship. For various reasons, toward the end of the last decade there was a lively increase in the 'need' for censorship in Bitinia; in just a few years, the existing central offices had to double their staff and establish local branches in almost all the provincial capitals. Difficulties were encountered, however, in recruiting the necessary personnel: first, because the work of a censor is, as is well known, arduous and subtle, requiring specialized training that even otherwise highly qualified people lack;

and, second, because, according to recent statistics, the actual practice of censorship can be dangerous.

I do not mean to allude here to the immediate risk of retaliation, which the efficient Bitinese police have reduced almost to nil. This is something different: careful medical studies conducted in the workplace have brought to light a specific type of professional hazard, irksome in nature and apparently irreversible, called by its discoverer 'paroxysmal dysthymia,' or 'Gowelius's disease.' The initial clinical picture is vague and ill defined; then, as the years pass, various sensory-system troubles appear (diplopia, olfactory and auditory disorders, exaggerated reactions to, for example, certain colors or flavors), which regularly develop, after remissions and relapses, into serious psychological anomalies and perversions.

Consequently, and despite offers of high wages, the number of applicants for these government jobs rapidly decreased, and the workload of the existing career functionaries increased accordingly, until it rose to unprecedented levels. In the censorship offices, work pending (screenplays, scores, manuscripts, illustrated works, advertising posters) accumulated in such huge proportions that not only were the assigned storage spaces chockablock with documents but so were lobbies, corridors, and bathrooms as well. One case was reported of a division manager who, after an avalanche of files fell on him, died of suffocation before help arrived.

At first, mechanization provided a solution. Each branch was equipped with modern electronic systems: since I have only a basic knowledge of such things I am unable to describe with any precision how they worked, but I was told that their magnetic memory contained three distinct lists of words, *hints, plots, topics*,* and frames of reference. Anything that corresponded to the first list was automatically deleted from the work under examination; anything on the second led to elimination of the entire work; anything on the third meant the immediate arrest and death by hanging of the author and the publisher.

The results were optimum with regard to processing the amount of work (in a few days the storage spaces in the offices were cleared), but in terms of quality they proved inadequate. There were outrageous cases of oversight: *Diary of a Sparrow*, by Claire Efrem, was 'approved' and published, and it sold with incredible success, and yet the book was of dubious literary merit and patently immoral, the author having used blatantly

---

* In English in original.

transparent techniques to disguise through allusion and paraphrase all the most offensive aspects of today's ethics. Conversely, witness the sad case of Tuttle: Colonel Tuttle, the acclaimed critic and military historian, was forced to climb the gallows because in one of his volumes on the Caucasus campaign, owing to a simple mistake, the word 'brigadier' appeared in altered form as 'brassiere' and was recognized by the office of mechanized censorship in Issarvan as an obscene reference. The author of a modest manual on animal husbandry miraculously escaped the same tragic fate because he had the means to flee abroad, whence he petitioned the Consulate before the court was able to pass sentence.

To these three episodes, which came to public attention, must be added numerous others, rumors of which spread by word of mouth but which were ignored by the officials because (as is obvious) any information about them fell, in its turn, under the censor's knife. A crisis situation erupted, resulting in a near total defection of the country's cultural forces: a situation that, despite a few feeble attempts at reversal, persists today.

There is, however, recent news that gives rise to some hope. A physiologist, whose name is being withheld, concluded one of his in-depth studies by revealing in a much discussed paper some new facets of the psychology of domestic animals. If pets are subjected to particular conditioning, they can not only learn simple jobs involving transport and organization but also make actual decisions.

Without a doubt, this is a vast and fascinating field, offering practically unlimited possibilities: to summarize what has been published in the Bitinese press up to the time of this writing, the work of censorship, which is damaging to the human brain, and is performed in far too rigid a manner by machines, could be profitably entrusted to animals trained for the purpose. Seriously considered, this disconcerting idea is not in itself absurd: in the last analysis, it is only a matter of decisions.

Curiously, the mammals closest to humans were found to be least useful for the task. Dogs, monkeys, and horses who underwent the conditioning proved to be poor judges precisely because they were too intelligent and sensitive. According to our anonymous scholar, they act far too passionately; they respond in unpredictable ways to the slightest foreign stimuli, which are inevitable in every workplace; they exhibit strange preferences, perhaps congenital but still inexplicable, for certain mental categories; and their own memories are uncontrollable and excessive. In sum, they reveal in these circumstances an *esprit de finesse* that would be detrimental to the goals of censorship.

Surprising results, on the other hand, were obtained

with the common barnyard chicken: this animal's success is such that, as is common knowledge, four experimental offices have already been entrusted to teams of hens, under the control and supervision of experienced functionaries, naturally. The hens, besides being easily procured and costing little, both as an initial investment and for their subsequent maintenance, are capable of making rapid and definitive decisions. They stick scrupulously to the prescribed mental programs, and, given their cold, calm nature and their evanescent memory, they are not subject to distractions.

The general opinion around here is that in a few years the method will be extended to all the censorship offices in the country.

Approved by the censor.

Knall

It's not the first time something like this has happened here: a habit, or an object, or an idea becomes, within a few weeks, almost universally widespread, without the newspapers or the mass media having anything to do with it. There was the craze for the yo-yo, then for Chinese mushrooms, then Pop art, Zen Buddhism, the hula-hoop. Now it is time for the knall.

No one knows who invented it, but, to judge from the price (a four-inch knall costs the equivalent of 3,000 lire or a little more), it doesn't contain much in the way of costly materials or inventive genius or *software*.* I bought one myself, down at the port, right in front of a cop, who didn't bat an eyelash. Of course I have no intention of using it. I just wanted to see how it works and how it's constructed: it seems a legitimate curiosity.

* In English in original.

A knall is a small, smooth cylinder, as long and thick as a Tuscan cigar, and not much heavier: it is sold loose or in boxes of twenty. Some are solid-colored, gray or red, but the majority come in wrappers printed with revoltingly tasteless little scenes and comic figures, in the style of decorations on jukeboxes and pinball machines: a bare-breasted girl fires a knall at her suitor's enormous rear end; a pair of tiny Max and Moritz types with insolent expressions, chased by a furious farmer, turn at the last minute, knalls in hand, and the pursuer falls backward, kicking his long, booted legs in the air.

Nothing is known about the mechanism by which the knall kills, or at least nothing about it has been published to date. *Knall*, in German, means crack, bang, crash; *abknallen*, in the slang of the Second World War, came to mean 'kill with a firearm,' whereas the firing of a knall is typically silent. Maybe the name – unless it has a completely different origin, or is an abbreviation – alludes to the moment of death, which in effect is instantaneous: the person who is struck – even if only superficially, on the hand or on the ear – falls lifeless immediately, and the corpse shows no sign of trauma, except for a small ring-shaped bruise at the point of contact, along the knall's geometric axis.

A knall can be used only once, then is thrown away. This is a neat, clean town, and knalls are not usually found on the sidewalks but only in the garbage cans on street corners and at tram stops. Exploded knalls are darker and more flaccid than unused ones; they are easily recognizable. It's not that they've all been employed for criminal purposes: fortunately, we are still a long way from this. But in certain circles carrying a knall – quite openly, in a breast pocket, or attached to the belt, or behind one ear the way a pork butcher carries a pencil – has become de rigueur. Now, since knalls have an expiration date, like antibiotics or film, many people feel obliged to fire them before they expire, not so much out of prudence as because the firing of a knall has unusual effects, which, though they have been described and studied only in part, are already widely known among consumers. It shatters stone and cement and in general all solid materials – the harder the material the more easily. It pierces wood and paper, sometimes setting them on fire; it melts metals; in water it creates a tiny steaming whirlpool, which, however, disappears immediately. In addition, with a skillfully directed shot one can light a cigarette or even a pipe – a bravura move that, in spite of the disproportionate expense, many young people practice, precisely because of the risk involved. In fact, it has been suggested that this is why the majority of knalls are used for lawful purposes.

The knall is undoubtedly a handy device: it isn't

metal, and hence its presence is not detected by common magnetic instruments or X rays; it weighs and costs little; its action is silent, swift, and sure; it's very easy to dispose of. Some psychologists, however, insist that these qualities are not sufficient to explain the knall's proliferation. They maintain that its use would be limited to criminal and terrorist circles if setting it off required a simple movement, such as pressure or friction; however, the knall goes off only if it is maneuvered in a particular way, a precise and rhythmic sequence of twists in one direction and then the other – an operation, in short, that requires skill and dexterity, a little like unlocking the combination of a safe. This operation, it should be noted, is only hinted at but not described in the instructions for use that accompany every box. Therefore, shooting the knall is the object of a secret rite in which initiates indoctrinate neophytes, a rite that has taken on a ceremonial and esoteric character, and is performed in cleverly camouflaged clubs. We might recall here, as an extreme case, the grim discovery that was made in April by the police in F.: in the basement of a restaurant a group of fifteen twelve-year-old boys and a youth of twenty-three were found dead, all clutching in their right hand a discharged knall, and all displaying on the tip of the left ring finger the typical circular bruise.

The police believe that it's better not to draw too much attention to the knall, because doing so would only encourage its spread: this seems to me a questionable opinion, springing, perhaps, from the considerable impotence of the police themselves. At the moment, the only means at their disposal for aid in capturing the biggest knall distributors, whose profits must be monstrous, are informers and anonymous telephone calls.

Being hit by a knall is certainly fatal, but only at close range; beyond a meter, it's completely harmless, and doesn't even hurt. This feature has had some unusual consequences. Movie-going has decreased significantly, because audience habits have changed: those who go to the movies, alone or in groups, leave at least two seats between them and the other spectators, and, if this isn't possible, often they prefer to turn in their tickets. The same thing happens on the trams, on the subways, and in the stadiums: people, in short, have developed a 'crowd reflex,' similar to that of many animals, who can't bear the close proximity of others of their kind. Also, the behavior of people on the streets has changed: many prefer to remain at home, or to stay off the sidewalks, thus exposing themselves to other dangers, or obstructing traffic. Many, meeting face to face in hallways or on sidewalks, avoid going around each other, resisting each other like magnetic poles.

The experts have not shown excessive concern about the dangers connected with the widespread use of the knall. They would observe that this device does not spill blood, which is reassuring. In fact, it's indisputable that the great majority of men feel the need, acute or chronic, to kill their neighbor or themselves, but it's not a matter of generic killing: in every instance they have the desire 'to shed blood,' 'to wash away with blood' their own infamy or that of others, 'to give their blood' to their country or other institutions. Those who strangle (themselves) or poison (themselves) are much less highly esteemed. In brief, blood, along with fire and wine, is at the center of a grand, glowing-red emotional nexus, vivid in a thousand dreams, poems, and idiomatic expressions: it is sacred and profane, and in its presence man, like the bull and the shark, becomes agitated and fierce. Now, precisely because the knall kills without bloodshed, it's doubtful that it will last. Perhaps that's why, in spite of its obvious advantages, it has not, so far, become a danger to society.

Gladiators

Nicola would happily have stayed home, and even in bed until ten, but Stefania wouldn't hear of it. At eight, she was already on the phone: she reminded him that he had been making excuses for far too long. Sometimes it was the rain, sometimes it was the contestants, who were mediocre, sometimes he had to go to a meeting, and sometimes there were his silly humanitarian excuses. Noticing in his voice a shadow of reluctance, or, perhaps, only of a bad mood, she ended by telling him outright that promises are made to be kept. She was a girl with many virtues, but when she got an idea in her head there was no way around it. Nicola didn't recall having made her an actual promise. He had said, vaguely, that yes, someday they would go to the stadium – all his colleagues went, and also (alas!) all her colleagues. Every Friday they filled in betting forms for the gladiator contest, and he had agreed with her that one shouldn't set oneself apart, give oneself the airs of an intellectual; and then it was an experience, a curiosity that, once in your life, you needed to satisfy, otherwise you don't know the world you're living in. Yet now that it had come to the point, he realized that he had made all those speeches with some mental reservation – he had no desire to actually see the gladiators and never would. On the other hand, how to say no to Stefania? He would pay dearly, he knew: with insults, sulks, rebuffs. Maybe even worse – there was that fair-haired cousin of his . . .

He shaved, washed, dressed, went out. The streets were deserted, but there was already a line at the store on Via San Secondo. He hated lines, but he got on the end of it just the same. The advertisement was hanging on the wall, in the usual garish colors. There were six entrants; the names of the gladiators meant nothing to him, except that of Turi Lorusso, Not that he knew much about Lorusso's technique; he knew that he was good, that he was paid an enormous sum, that he slept with a countess, and perhaps also with the relevant count, that he gave a lot to charity and paid no taxes. While Nicola waited his turn, he listened in on the conversations of his neighbors.

'If you ask me, after thirty years they shouldn't allow it anymore . . .'

'Of course, the acceleration, the eyes aren't what they

used to be, but, on the other hand, he has experience of the arena that . . .'

'But did you see him, in '91, against that madman who drove the Mercedes? When he threw the hammer from twenty meters and hit him straight on? And remember the time they ejected him for . . .?'

He bought two tickets for the grandstand: it wasn't the moment to worry about cost. He went home and telephoned Stefania: he would pick her up at two.

By three the stadium was full. The first entry was scheduled for three, but still at three-thirty nothing had happened. Near them sat a white-haired old man with a deep tan. Nicola asked him if the delay was normal.

'They always make you wait. It's incredible – they act like prima donnas. In my time it was different. Instead of foam-rubber bumpers there were beaks – no nonsense. It was hard to escape without injury. Only the top players managed it, the ones who were born with combat in their blood. You're young, you don't remember the champions who came out of Pinerolo's stable, and, even better, Alpignano's. Now, can you believe it? They're all from reformatories or from the New Prisons, or even from the prison for the criminally insane: if they accept, their sentence is commuted. It's laughable now, they have insurance, disability, paid holidays, and after fifty fights they even get a pension. Oh, yes, there are some who retire at forty.'

A murmur rose from the bleachers, and the first man entered. He was very young: he appeared confident but you could see he was afraid. Immediately afterward a flame-red Fiat 127 came into the ring; the three ritual honks of the horn sounded, and Nicola felt the nervous grip of Stefania's hand on his biceps; the car aimed straight at the boy, who waited in a slight crouch, tense, legs wide, gripping the hammer convulsively in his fist. Suddenly the auto accelerated, its tractor wheels spewing two jets of sand in its wake. The boy dodged and struck a blow, but too late: the hammer just grazed the side, denting it slightly. The driver must not have had much imagination; there were several more such charges, extremely monotonous, then the gong sounded and the round concluded with no decision.

The second gladiator (Nicola glanced at the program) was called Blitz, and he was stocky and smooth-skinned. There were several skirmishes with the Alfasud compact car that he had drawn as an adversary; the man was skillful enough and managed to keep wide of it for two or three minutes, then the car hit him, in first gear but hard, and he was thrown a dozen meters. His head was bleeding; the doctor came, declared him incapacitated, and the stretcher-bearers carried him off amid the catcalls of the spectators. Nicola's neighbor was outraged. He said that Blitz, whose real name, by the way, was Craveri, was an impostor, that he got himself injured on purpose, that he should change careers – in fact, the Federation should change careers for him: take away his license and put him back in the ranks of the unemployed.

In the case of the third, who was also up against an economy car, a Renault 4, he pointed out that these cars were more dangerous than the big heavy cars. 'If it was up to me, I would make them all Mini Morrises. They have acceleration, and they handle well. With those monsters of 1600 and up, nothing ever happens. They're fine for newcomers – just smoke in their eyes.' At the third charge, the gladiator waited for the auto without moving: at the last instant he threw himself flat on the ground and the car drove over him without touching him. The spectators shouted with enthusiasm; many of the women threw flowers and purses into the arena, and even a shoe, but Nicola learned that that move, though it looked impressive, wasn't really dangerous. It was called 'the Rudolf,' because a gladiator named Rudolf had invented it: he had later become famous, had had a political career, and was now a big shot on the Olympic Committee.

Next, there was the usual comic interlude: a duel between two forklifts. They were the same model and color but one had a red stripe painted on it and the other a green stripe. Because they were so heavy, they were difficult to maneuver, sinking into the sand almost up to their hubs. In vain they tried to push each other back, with their forks entwined like battling stags; then the green stripe disentangled itself, backed up rapidly, and, making a tight turn, butted the side of red with its rear. Red yielded but then quickly went into reverse and managed to lodge its fork under the belly of green. The fork rose, and green swayed and then fell on one side, indecently exposing its differential and muffler. The audience laughed and applauded.

The fourth gladiator had to go against a banged-up Peugeot. The crowd immediately began to shout 'Rigged!' The driver even had the audacity to switch on his turn signal before swerving.

The fifth entry was a real spectacle. The gladiator was gutsy and was obviously aiming not just at the windshield but at the head of the driver, and he missed by a hair. He dodged three charges, with precision and lazy grace, not even raising the hammer; at the fourth, he bounced up in front of the car like a spring, came down on the hood, and with two brutal hammer blows shattered the windshield. Nicola heard a brief, strangled cry that stood out from the roar of the crowd: it was Stefania, who was pressed tight against him. The driver seemed to be blinded: instead of braking, he accelerated and hit the wooden barrier sideways; the car rebounded and came to rest on its side, trapping one of the gladiator's feet in the sand. He was mad with rage, and continued, through the empty frame of the windshield, to pound the head of the driver, who was trying to get out of the car by the door facing up. Finally he emerged, his face bleeding; he tore the hammer away from the gladiator, and began wringing his neck. The crowd yelled a word that Nicola couldn't understand, but his neighbor calmly explained to him that they were asking the director of the competition to spare his life, which in fact was what happened. A tow truck from the automobile club entered the arena, and in a flash the car was turned rightside up and towed away. The driver and the gladiator shook hands amid the applause, and then walked toward the locker rooms waving, but after a few steps the gladiator staggered and fell. It wasn't clear if he was dead or had only fainted. They loaded him, too, onto the tow truck.

As the great Lorusso entered the arena, Nicola realized that Stefania had turned very pale. He felt a vague rancor toward her, and he would have liked to stay longer, if only to make her pay – he couldn't care less about Lorusso. On principle he would have preferred Stefania to ask him if they could leave, but he knew her, and knew that she would never stoop to that, so he told her that he had had enough, and they left. Stefania didn't feel well, she felt like throwing up, but when he questioned her she said curtly that it was the sausage she had eaten at dinner. She refused to have a glass of bitters at the bar, refused to spend the evening with him, rebuffed every topic of conversation that he suggested: she really must be ill. Nicola took her home, and realized that he, too, had little appetite, and didn't even feel like playing the usual game of pool with Renato. He drank two cognacs and went to bed.

The Fugitive

To compose a poem that is worth reading and remembering is a gift of destiny: it happens to only a few people, without regard for rules or intentions, and to them it happens only a few times in their lives. Perhaps this is a good thing; if the phenomenon were more frequent, we would be drowning in poetic messages, our own and those of others, to the detriment of us all. To Pasquale, too, it had happened only a few times, and the awareness of having a poem in his mind, ready to be caught in flight and fixed on a page like a butterfly, had always been accompanied by a curious sensation, by an aura like that which precedes epileptic fits: each time, he had heard a faint whistle in his ears, and a ticklish shiver ran through him from head to foot.

In a few moments the whistle and the shiver disappeared, and he found himself clear-headed, with the core of the poem lucid and distinct; he had only to write it down, and, lo and behold, the other lines hastened to crowd around it, obedient and strong. In a quarter of an hour the work was done: but this flash, this instantaneous process in which conception and birth succeeded one another almost like lightning and thunder, had been granted to Pasquale only five or six times in his life. Luckily, he wasn't a poet by profession: he had a dull, boring office job.

He felt the symptoms described above after two years of silence, as he was sitting at his desk, examining an insurance policy. In fact, he felt them with an unusual intensity: the whistle was penetrating and the shiver was a nearly convulsive tremor, which disappeared immediately, leaving him with a sensation of vertigo. The key verse was there before him, as if written on the wall, or, rather, inside his skull. His colleagues at the neighboring desks didn't notice anything. Pasquale concentrated fiercely on the sheet of paper in front of him: from the core the poem radiated out through all his senses like a growing organism, and soon it was before him; it seemed to be throbbing, just like a living thing.

It was the most beautiful poem that Pasquale had ever written. There it was, right before his eyes, without a correction, the handwriting tall, elegant, and smooth: it was almost as if the sheet of copy paper on which it was written had difficulty bearing its weight, like a column too slender beneath the burden of a giant statue.

It was six o'clock: Pasquale locked the poem in his drawer and went home. It seemed to him that he deserved a reward, and on the way he bought himself an ice cream.

The next morning he rushed to the office. He was impatient to reread the poem, because he was well aware how hard it is to judge a newly written work: the value and the meaning, or the lack of value and meaning, become clear only the morning after. He opened the drawer and didn't see the page: and yet he was sure that he had left it on top of all the other papers. He dug around among them, frantically at first, then methodically, but he had to admit that the poem had disappeared. He searched the other drawers, and then he realized that the poem was right there in front of him, on the in-box tray. What tricks distraction plays! But how could he not be distracted, in the face of the ultimate work of his life?

Pasquale was certain that his future biographers would remember him for nothing else: only for that 'Annunciation.' He reread it and was enthusiastic, almost in love. He was about to take it to the photocopying machine when the boss called him in; he kept him for an hour and a half, and when Pasquale returned to his desk the copier was broken. By four o'clock the electrician had repaired it, but the photocopying paper was all used up. For that day there was nothing to be done: recalling the incident of the previous evening, Pasquale placed the sheet of paper in the drawer with great care. He closed it, then changed his mind and opened it, and finally he closed it again and left. The next day the piece of paper wasn't there.

This business was becoming annoying. Pasquale turned all his drawers upside down, bringing to light papers that had been forgotten for decades: as he searched, he tried to retrieve in memory if not the whole composition at least that first line, that nucleus which had enlightened him, but he couldn't: in fact, he had the precise sensation that he never would. He was different, different from that moment on: he was no longer the same Pasquale, and he never would be again, just as a dead man does not return to life, and you never put your foot in the same river twice. There was a nauseating metallic taste in his mouth: the taste of frustration, of nevermore. Disconsolate, he sat down in his office chair, and saw the page stuck to the wall, to his left, a little distance from his head. It was obvious: some colleague had intended to play a tasteless trick; perhaps someone had been spying on him and was on to his secret.

He seized the sheet of paper by one edge and detached it from the wall, encountering almost no resistance: the author of the trick must have used a poor-quality paste, or used very little. He noticed that the other side of the paper was slightly grainy. He put it under his desk pad, and for the entire morning made excuses not to leave his desk, but when the noon whistle sounded, and everyone got up to go to lunch, Pasquale saw that the sheet of paper was sticking out from under the desk pad by a good inch. He took it out, folded it in fourths, and put it in his wallet: after all, there was no reason not to take it home. He would copy it by hand, or take it to the copy shop; that would solve the problem.

He reread the poem in the evening as he was going home on the subway. Contrary to what he usually felt, it seemed perfect: not a line or a syllable had to be changed. Still, before showing it to Gloria he would think about it. Everyone knows how a judgment can change even in a short time: Monday's masterpiece becomes insipid on Thursday, or even vice versa. He locked the sheet of paper in his private drawer, in the bedroom; but the following morning, when he opened his eyes, he saw it above him, stuck to the ceiling. Two-thirds of it was adhering to the plaster; the other third was hanging down.

Pasquale got the ladder and cautiously removed the piece of paper; again, when he felt it, the surface was rough, especially on the back. He touched it with his lips: there was no doubt, sticking out from the page were some tiny bumps, which seemed to be in rows. He took a magnifying glass and saw that it was so. Tiny hairs were sticking out from the page, corresponding to attributes of the letters on the other side. In particular, the extremities stuck out, the legs of the 'd's and the 'p's, and, above all, the little legs of the 'n's and of the 'm's; for example, behind the title, 'Annunciation,' the eight legs of the four 'n's could be clearly seen. They stuck out like the whiskers of a badly shaved beard, and it seemed to Pasquale that they even vibrated slightly.

It was time to go to the office, and Pasquale was perplexed. He didn't know where to put the poem. He realized that, for some reason, perhaps precisely because of its uniqueness, because of the life that openly animated it, the poem was trying to escape, to get away from him. He decided to observe it from close up: never mind the office – for once he would be late. Under the magnifying glass he could see that some of the attributes of the letters were surrounded by a thin, clear inlay, in the form of a narrow, elongated U, and were folded back, toward the other side of the paper, in such a way that, if you placed the piece of paper on the surface of the desk, it remained elevated a millimeter or two: he bent down to look, and he could distinctly see the light between the page and the desktop.

And he saw something more: as he watched, the sheet of paper moved in the direction of the title, away from him. It advanced a few millimeters a second, with a slow but uniform and assured motion. He turned it around, so that the title faced away from him; after a few seconds the page took up its march, this time in reverse, that is, toward the opposite edge of the desk.

By now it was getting late; Pasquale had an important appointment at nine-thirty, and he could delay no longer. He went to the storage closet, found a strip of plywood, got the paste, and pasted the wood on top of the piece of paper: 'Annunciation' was his work, in the end – his thing, his property. It remained to be seen who was stronger. He went to the office in a rage, and was unable to calm down even in the course of the delicate negotiations that he was in charge of, so that he conducted them in a rude and clumsy manner, and ended up with a deal that was decidedly mediocre, which, naturally, only increased his rage and ill humor. He felt like a race horse yoked to a mill wheel: after two days of walking in a circle are you still a race horse? Do you still have the desire to run, to be first at the finish line? No, you have a desire for silence, rest, and the stable. Luckily at home, at the stable, the poem awaited him. It would no longer escape: how could it?

It had not in fact escaped. He found the remains of it

stuck to the piece of wood: twenty little fragments, each no bigger than a postage stamp, for a total area no more than a fifth of the original sheet of paper. The rest of 'Annunciation' had departed, in the form of scraps, tiny crumpled, frayed shreds, which were scattered in all the corners of the house: he found only three or four, and though he smoothed them out carefully, they were illegible.

Pasquale spent the following Sunday in less and less reliable efforts to reconstruct the poem. From that time on, there were neither whistles nor shivers; he tried many times, during the rest of his life, to call to memory the lost text; in fact, at increasingly rare intervals, he wrote other versions of it, but they were increasingly thin, bloodless, and weak.

Bureau of Vital Statistics

There were four elevators, but one, as usual, was out of service. It wasn't always the same one and even the sign hanging on the door wasn't always the same. This one, for instance, said 'Out of Service'; others might say 'Not Working' or 'Broken' or 'Don't Touch' or even 'Back Soon.' Maybe it was the doorman, or the superintendent, who changed the signs according to some vaguely ironic whim. There were lines in front of the three other elevators, and this, too, happened every day, at the beginning and at the end of the workday. If his office hadn't been on the ninth floor, Arrigo would have taken the stairs; sometimes he did anyway, for the exercise, but that morning he felt a little tired.

The elevator finally arrived, and it was already full of employees coming from the basement and the sub-basement. Arrigo made his way in energetically but without shoving. The elevator rose, stopping with a jerk at every floor, and people got on and off, greeting each other distractedly. On the ninth floor, Arrigo himself got off and punched his time card. For two years now there had been a time clock on every floor. It had been a sensible innovation. Previously, there had been only one, on the ground floor, which always caused a terrible bottleneck, partly because there was little discipline, and people tried to push in front of you. In the office, people were already at their desks. Arrigo sat at his post, pulled the color photograph of his wife and their little girl out of the top drawer, and from the second drawer took writing supplies and the index cards left over from the previous day. This was the result of one of the boss's obsessions: at the end of the day, all the desks had to be cleared. Who knows why, certainly not for cleaning, because the desks were cleaned only two or three times a year: if you didn't want dust on your desk, you had to clean it yourself.

Arrigo's job was administrative in nature. Every day, he received a packet of index cards from the floor above. Each card contained the name of a human being and the date of his or her death; Arrigo had only to specify the cause. He would often get angry, for various reasons. The expiration date wasn't always the same: it could be years ahead, or months or days, for no apparent reason, and he felt that this was an injustice. Nor did it seem reasonable that there were no rules regarding age: some days he was handed hundreds of cards for newborns. Then, the boss complained if Arrigo kept to generic formulas: the man must be a sadist or a fan of crime news. It wasn't enough for Arrigo to write 'accident.' He wanted all the details and was never satisfied. He always demanded a correlation between the data on the cards and the cause of death, and this often embarrassed Arrigo.

The first index card of the day wasn't a problem. It bore the name of Yen Ch'ing-Hsu, fifty-eight years old, single, born in Han Tou, where he still resided, dockworker, no illnesses to speak of. Arrigo had no idea where Han Tou was: if he were to check the atlas every time, he'd never get anything done. Yen still had thirty-six days to live and Arrigo imagined him against the backdrop of an exotic sunset, sitting on a roll of cable before a turbid sea the color of a ripe banana; he was exhausted by his daily work, sad and alone. A man like this doesn't fear death and doesn't seek it, either, but he may act carelessly. Arrigo thought about it for a moment and then had him fall from a scaffold: he wouldn't suffer much.

Pedro Gonzales de Eslava didn't give him much trouble, either. In spite of the pompous name, he must have been a poor devil – he drank, had been involved in many fights among illegal immigrants, was forty-six years old, and had worked on half a dozen farms in the far south. He had five more months and would leave behind four children, who, however, lived with his wife and not with him. The wife was Puerto Rican, like Pedro; she was young, and she also worked. Arrigo consulted the medical encyclopedia and came up with hepatitis.

He was studying the third index card when Fernanda called him on the phone. She had seen in the paper that *Metropolis* was playing at some art house cinema; why not go see it tonight? Arrigo didn't like being interrupted at work and was noncommittal. The third index card was fairly obvious; everyone knows what happens to a man who races motorbikes. No one was forcing him to do it; he had only to choose a different profession – in cases like this, there's no need to have scruples. But he felt obliged to provide the details of the fatal accident and the hospital record.

He had no sympathy for Pierre-Jean La Motte. He was born in Lyons, but at the age of thirty-two he was already a full professor of political science at the University of Rio: evidently he was a man with connections. He had only twenty days to live, though he was in excellent health and played tennis every morning. Arrigo was racking his brains for an appropriate cause of death for La Motte when Lorusso came by and invited him to go for coffee. Arrigo went down with him to the vending machines on the fourth floor. Lorusso was dull. He had a son who wasn't doing well in math, and Arrigo thought that, with a father like that, it would be surprising if the son were a prodigy. Then Lorusso started to complain about his wife, who spent too much money, and about the heat that didn't work.

The coffee machine didn't work well, either. Lorusso banged on it and at long last it spat out two cups of coffee, pale and insipid but boiling hot. As Arrigo forced himself to gulp down the coffee, scalding his throat, Lorusso talked on about the paycheck that always came late and the deductions that were always too high. Finally, back at his desk, Arrigo squashed Pierre-Jean like a worm: brain hemorrhage – that'll teach him.

At around ten, Arrigo was finished with the cards left over from the previous day, but the office boy had already put the new cards on his desk. The first was all crumpled, maybe by the dating machine: he could make out only that it was for a person of the female sex, by the name of Adelia. Arrigo put the card aside, so much the better for Adelia: it's always useful to gain time. At any rate, he might decide to write a report: more and more often it happens that the first card of each packet is damaged . . . a regrettable occurrence . . . will maintenance please take care of it . . . sincerely yours. Instead he paused over the next card. Karen Kvarna, aged eight, born in Slidre, a mountain village in the heart of Norway. Karen, only child, illnesses N.A. (not available), student, was to die the following day. Arrigo was stuck. He imagined her flaxen-haired, kind, cheerful, serene, against the backdrop of solemn, immaculate mountains: if she had to die, then it would be without him, he would not take part in this. He grabbed the card and knocked on the boss's door: he heard a grumbled 'Come in,' entered, and said that it was a disgrace. That the work was poorly organized, that the purchase of the randomizer had been an idiotic idea, that the cards were full of mistakes – for example, this one right here. That they were all sheep and careerists and no one dared protest and no one took the job seriously. That he had had enough, that he couldn't care less about promotion, and that he wanted to be transferred.

The boss must have been expecting a scene from Arrigo for quite a while, because he gave no sign of surprise or indignation. Perhaps he was even glad to be rid of a programmer with such an unstable character. He told Arrigo to stop by again the next day. And the next day he gave him his transfer orders and made him sign two or three explanatory documents. Thus Arrigo found himself demoted from grade 7 to grade 6 and transferred to a small office in the attic of the building, in charge of determining the shape of the noses of newborns.

Buffet Dinner

Immediately upon entering through the front door, Innaminka felt uneasy and regretted having accepted the invitation. There was a butler of sorts, with a green sash around his belly, who took people's coats. Innaminka, whose coat was part of his body, shivered and felt dizzy at the thought that someone might take it from him. But there was more: behind the butler rose a great spiral staircase of beautiful polished black wood, broad and majestic but unmanageable. Unmanageable for him, that is. The other guests mounted it with ease, while he didn't dare even try. He kept turning in circles, embarrassed, waiting till no one was looking. On level ground he was good, but the length of his hindquarters alone was an obstacle – his feet were more or less twice as long as the stairs were deep. He waited a little more, sniffing at the walls and trying to appear indifferent, and once everyone else was upstairs he endeavored to go up as well.

He tried different methods: grabbing the banister with his front legs, or bending over and trying to climb on all fours, even employing his tail – but actually it was the tail, more than anything else, that got in the way. He ended up climbing clumsily sideways, placing his feet lengthwise on each step, his tail folded ignobly over his back. It took him a full ten minutes.

Upstairs was a long, narrow room, with a table placed crosswise; there were paintings on the walls, some depicting human or animal forms, others depicting nothing. Along the walls, and scattered around the floor, were bronze or marble figures that Innaminka found pleasing and vaguely familiar. The room was already crowded, but more people kept arriving: the men were in evening attire, the women wore long black dresses and were bedecked with jewels, their eyelids painted green or blue. Innaminka hesitated for a moment and then, sidling along the wall and avoiding abrupt movements, took refuge in a corner. The other guests looked at him with mild curiosity. In passing, he overheard a few casual comments: 'He's pretty, isn't he?' '. . . no, he doesn't have one, dear. Can't you see he's a male?' 'I heard on TV that they are almost extinct. . . . No, not for the fur, which isn't worth much anyway. It's because they destroy the crops.'

★

After a while, the young hostess emerged from a group of guests and came toward him. She was very thin, with large, wide-set gray eyes and an expression between annoyance and surprise, as if someone had brusquely woken her up at that very moment. She told him that she had heard a lot about him, and this Innaminka found hard to believe: maybe it was just a form of greeting, and she said it to all her guests. She asked him if he'd like something to eat or drink: she didn't seem very intelligent, but she probably had a kind heart, and it was precisely because of her kindness rather than her intelligence that she realized that Innaminka understood her fairly well but could not answer her, and she moved on.

Actually, Innaminka was hungry and thirsty: not to an unbearable degree, but enough to make him uncomfortable. Now, the dinner was one of those melancholy buffet affairs, where you have to choose what you want from a distance, craning between heads and shoulders, find the plates, find the silverware and the paper napkins, get in line, reach the table, serve yourself, and then back away, making sure not to spill anything, either on yourself or on anyone else. Besides, he could see neither grass nor hay on the table: there was a rather appetizing-looking salad, and peas in a brown sauce, but as Innaminka hesitated, debating whether or not to get in line, the one dish and then the other were finished. Innaminka gave up. He turned his back on the table and, proceeding with care through the crowd, tried to return to his corner. He thought with loving nostalgia of his wife, and of his youngest, who was growing up: he was a good jumper and went out to pasture by himself, but now and then he still demanded to return to his mother's pouch – indeed, he was a little spoiled, and liked to spend the night in that warm darkness.

During his laborious retreat, he encountered several waiters who carried trays and offered glasses of wine and orangeade and canapés that looked tempting. He didn't even think about taking a glass in the middle of the crowd, while everyone was bumping into him. He gathered up his courage, grabbed a canapé, and brought it to his mouth, but it instantly fell apart in his fingers, so that he had to lick them one by one and then lick his lips and whiskers for a long time. He looked around, suspicious, but no, no one was paying any attention. He crouched in his corner, and to pass the time he began to observe the guests closely, trying to imagine how they would behave, men and women, if they were being chased by a dog. No mistaking it – in those long wide skirts, the women would never get off the ground, and even the swiftest among the men, even with a good running start, wouldn't be able to jump a third of the distance that he could jump from a standstill. But you can never tell, maybe they were good at other things.

He was hot and thirsty, and at some point he realized with dismay that an increasingly urgent need was growing in him. He thought that it surely must happen to others, too, and for a few minutes he looked around to see how they dealt with it, but it seemed that no one else had his problem. So very slowly he approached a large pot in which a ficus tree grew, and pretending to sniff the leaves he sat astride the pot and relieved himself. The leaves were fresh and shiny and had a nice smell. Innaminka ate a couple and found them tasty but had to stop because he noticed a woman staring at him.

She stared at him and came closer. Innaminka realized that it was too late to pretend that nothing had happened and move away. She was young and had broad shoulders, massive bones, strong hands, a pale face, and clear eyes. To Innaminka, of course, her feet were of primary importance, but the woman's skirt was so long and her shoes so complicated that he couldn't get even an idea of their shape and length. For a moment he feared that the woman had noticed the business with the ficus tree and had come to reprimand him or punish him, but he soon realized that it wasn't so. She sat down on a small armchair beside him and started talking to him sweetly. Innaminka understood hardly anything she said, but at once he felt calmer; he lowered his ears and made himself more comfortable. The woman came even closer and began to caress him, first on the neck and back, then, seeing that he was closing his eyes, under his chin and on his chest, between his front paws, where there is that triangle of white fur that kangaroos are so proud of.

The woman talked and talked, in a subdued tone, as if she were afraid the others would hear. Innaminka understood that she was unhappy, that someone had behaved badly toward her, that this someone was, or had been, her man, that this event had occurred a short time ago, perhaps that very evening: but nothing more than that. Since he, too, was unhappy, he felt sympathetic toward the woman, and for the first time that evening he stopped wishing that the reception would soon be over; instead he hoped that the woman would continue to caress him and, in particular, that her hands would go lower and run lightly and knowingly along the mighty muscles of his tail and his thighs, of which he was even prouder than of his white triangle.

This, however, was not to be. The woman continued to caress him, but with increasing distraction, paying no attention to his shivers of pleasure, and continuing all the while to complain about certain human troubles of hers that seemed to Innaminka not to amount to much – to one man instead of another man whom she would have preferred. Innaminka thought that, if this was how things stood, the woman would do better to caress this second man instead of him; and that maybe that was exactly what she was doing; and furthermore that she was beginning to bore him, given that for at least a quarter of an hour she had been repeating the same caresses and the same words. In short, it was clear that she was thinking of herself and not of him.

Suddenly a man sprang out of the seething crowd, grabbed the woman's wrist, jerked her to her feet, and said something very unpleasant and brutal to her. He then dragged her away and she followed, without giving Innaminka so much as a farewell glance.

Innaminka had had enough. From his observation post he stretched up as high as he could, straightening his back and raising himself on his hind legs and tail as on a tripod, to see if anyone was starting to leave. He didn't want to attract attention by being the first. But as soon as he caught sight of an elegant elderly couple making the rounds to say their goodbyes and heading toward the cloakroom, Innaminka took off.

He negotiated the first few meters slinking between the legs of the guests, below the level of breasts and stomachs; he stayed low, supported alternately on his hind legs and on his front legs with the help of his tail. But when he was near the table, which by now had been cleared, he noticed that the floor on either side of the table was clear, too, and so he jumped right over it, feeling his lungs fill effortlessly with air and with joy. With a second leap he was at the head of the stairs: rushing, he miscalculated the distance and landed off-balance on the top steps. There was nothing for it but to descend that way, like a sack, half crawling and half rolling. But as soon as he reached the ground floor he hopped to his feet. Under the expressionless gaze of the doorman, he took a deep, voluptuous breath of the damp, grimy night air and immediately set off along Via Borgospesso, no longer in a rush, with long, happy, elastic leaps.

a little history

Penguin Modern Classics were launched in 1961, and have been shaping the reading habits of generations ever since.

The list began with distinctive grey spines and evocative pictorial covers – a look that, after various incarnations, continues to influence their current design – and with books that are still considered landmark classics today.

Penguin Modern Classics have caused scandal and political change, inspired great films and broken down barriers, whether social, sexual or the boundaries of language itself. They remain the most provocative, groundbreaking, exciting and revolutionary works of the last 100 years (or so).

In 2011, on the fiftieth anniversary of the Modern Classics, we're publishing fifty Mini Modern Classics: the very best short fiction by writers ranging from Beckett to Conrad, Nabokov to Saki, Updike to Wodehouse. Though they don't take long to read, they'll stay with you long after you turn the final page.

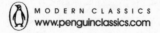

MODERN CLASSICS
www.penguinclassics.com